Raggedy Ann's Birthday Party Book

SIMON & SCHUSTER BOOKS FOR YOUNG READERS

An imprint of Simon & Schuster Children's Publishing Division

1230 Avenue of the Americas, New York, New York 10020

Book design by Jennifer Reyes

The text of this book is set in Venetian.

The illustrations are rendered in watercolor.

Printed in Hong Kong

10 9 8 7 6 5 4 3 2 1

CIP Data for this book is available from the Library of Congress.

ISBN 0-689-82850-0

Raggedy Ann's Birthday Party Book

By Elizabeth Silbaugh

Illustrated by Laura Francesca Filippucci

Simon & Schuster Books for Young Readers
New York   London   Toronto   Sydney   Singapore

One day, a beautiful new doll
arrived in Marcella's room, where
Raggedy Ann lived with all of the
other dolls. It was Marcella's birthday,
and the new doll had been a birthday
present. She had golden curls and a
pretty red mouth and round blue
eyes that actually opened and closed
when you tipped her back and forth.

When Marcella had put the new doll down and gone running back downstairs again, all the dolls gathered around to meet the newcomer.

"Welcome!" said Raggedy Ann. "I am Raggedy Ann. What is your name?"

The new doll turned her pretty smile to Raggedy Ann.

"I think my name is Clarissa," she said.

"What do you mean 'you think'?" asked Annabel-Lee and Thomas and Uncle Clem and all the other dolls at once.

"Well . . . Marcella named me only a little while ago. I am brand-new. She just opened me today because today is her birthday."

The other dolls looked confused. Then they looked to Raggedy Ann because she was the wisest and kindest doll of all.

"What is a birthday, Raggedy Ann?"

"Oh!" said Raggedy Ann. "Birthdays are such fun! Why, birthdays are the most wonderful things you can imagine."

The dolls sat spellbound as Raggedy Ann went on.

"Everyone has a birthday. *Your* birthday is your special day—the day of the year when you were born. Once a year, every year, when your birthday comes around, your friends and family celebrate the happy day when you first arrived!"

happy birthday

Just then, Raggedy Ann had a brilliant idea.

"Clarissa, because you have just arrived, today is *your* birthday! This will give us all a chance to see what birthdays are all about."

Do you know when your birthday is? What kinds of things do your family and friends do to make the day special for you? Let's see how Raggedy Ann and her friends give Clarissa a magnificent birthday!

"First off," said Raggedy Ann, "we need some time to get ready. Clarissa, you must be tired from all the excitement of being new. Why don't you take a nap while the rest of us work on the celebration? Besides, we want to surprise you with some fun things!"

"I *am* a bit sleepy," Clarissa replied with a yawn.

As Clarissa nestled down for a rest in the nursery, the others rolled up their sleeves and began to prepare.

Making birthday cards is an especially nice way to get in the mood for a birthday. Fold a sheet of blank paper, gather together some art supplies, and see what you can do! The dolls' own artwork and birthday wishes will make Clarissa feel extra happy.

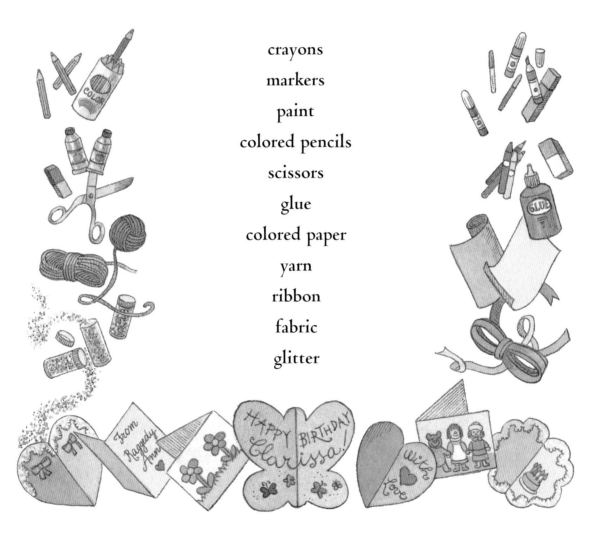

crayons
markers
paint
colored pencils
scissors
glue
colored paper
yarn
ribbon
fabric
glitter

"If this is going to be a proper birthday," said Raggedy Ann, "we certainly must make a birthday cake. Let's do that now so that it has time to bake!"

The dolls all loved birthday cake, and they were happy to help measure and pour and stir up the ingredients. Sliding the pans into the oven, they knew the delicious smell of cake would soon fill the house!

Cake mixes that come in boxes are easy to use and make very tasty cakes. If you want to jazz up your cake for a special birthday, here is Raggedy Ann's favorite recipe. Since you will have to chill the cake for a while, be sure to start early.

SUPER-SPECIAL STRIPEY CAKE

Ingredients:

1 boxed cake mix (white or yellow will work best)

Eggs, oil, and water called for on the back of the box

2 cups boiling water

2 small packets of flavored gelatin—your favorite colors!

Icing, whipped cream, or whipped topping

Directions:

Following the directions on the box, make the cake in two 8-inch or 9-inch round layers. After the cake has baked and while the layers are cooling on a rack, wash and dry the cake pans. When the layers have completely cooled, put them back into the pans. Prick the top of each layer with a fork about twenty times.

Next, pour each packet of gelatin powder into its own bowl. Ask an adult for help, and carefully stir 1 cup of boiling water into each color. Continue stirring until the powder has dissolved (this should take about 2 minutes). Pour the gelatin over the cake layers. You can make each layer a different color, or you can put some of each color on top of both layers. When you have used up all of the gelatin, put the cake layers, still in their pans, into the refrigerator for 3 hours.

When you are ready to frost the cake, ask an adult for help and fill the sink with about 1 inch of warm water. Set one pan in the water for about 10 seconds, then lift it out and wipe it dry. Unmold the cake layer onto a plate. Frost the top with icing or whipped topping. Set the second pan in the warm water, lift it out, dry it, and unmold the second cake layer on top of the first. Continue frosting until all sides are covered.

You will need to store the cake in the refrigerator because the gelatin will become runny in warm air. When it's time to celebrate, add candles, sing, and eat!

"What about presents?" asked Thomas when the dolls had finished wiping up the kitchen.

"Well," replied Raggedy Ann, "giving presents is a good way to show that you are glad that someone was born. Presents don't have to be fancy or expensive, though. In fact, homemade presents can be the best kind." So the dolls all set to work making presents for Clarissa.

Raggedy Ann braids a
bracelet out of yarn.

Thomas paints a picture on
a rock for a paperweight.

Uncle Clem makes a pencil
holder out of an empty can.

Annabel-Lee embroiders
a handkerchief.

Then the dolls wrapped their presents in tissue paper that they decorated themselves.

Try making patterns with markers or crayons. Or you can cut sponges into small shapes, dip them in poster paint, and then press them on the paper.

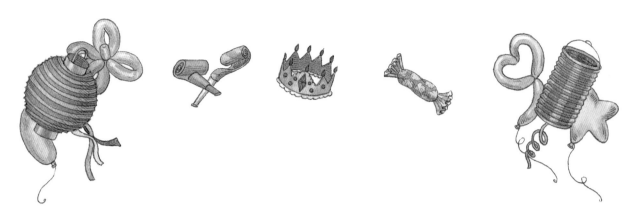

"Now for decorations!" said Raggedy Ann once all the presents had been wrapped and piled on the table. A birthday can be simple or fancy, but it is always nice to make the room look a bit different for the celebration.

The dolls bustled about decorating for Clarissa's birthday.

Thomas set the table with extra-pretty place mats and napkins.

"Annabel-Lee, will you help me blow up these balloons and hang them with the streamers?" asked Uncle Clem.

Meanwhile, Raggedy Ann made place cards to show where each person should sit. She had some party favors to set around the table, too.

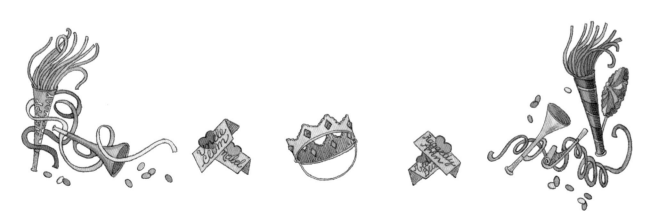

When everything was ready, the dolls tiptoed into the nursery.

"Happy birthday! Happy birthday!" they called gently, awakening their new friend. Clarissa opened her shiny blue eyes and smiled to see all the dolls gathered around her bed.

"These are for you," Annabel-Lee said as she handed Clarissa a beautiful bouquet of birthday flowers.

Raggedy Ann took Clarissa by the hand, and the dolls led her to the table.

"Oh, it's beautiful!" gasped Clarissa. "You did all this for me?"

"Yes! It's your birthday, and you are the birthday girl," said Raggedy Ann. She pulled out the chair at the head of the table, and Clarissa took a seat. The other dolls found their places and sat down, too.

When all the dolls were seated and admiring the decorations, Uncle Clem suddenly turned off the lights. The door to the kitchen swung open, and Raggedy Ann came in carrying the birthday cake! Clarissa's face glowed with happiness in the light of the candles as the dolls sang "Happy Birthday."

"Blow out the candles and make a wish, Clarissa! Wish for anything you like, but don't tell," explained Raggedy Ann.

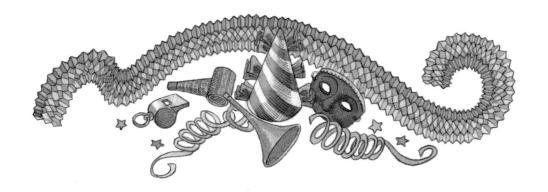

Every birthday party is different. Sometimes there are lots of friends, or just one or two. There can be a big family or a small one, and sometimes the birthday boy or girl gets to choose what will be served for dinner.

One thing all birthdays have in common is that they are special days. Your birthday is the day you became you!

Thomas helped Clarissa cut the cake so that everyone could have a piece with a scoop of ice cream on top. The dolls put on their party hats and made a good racket with their noisemakers. What a celebration!

"Open your cards and presents, Clarissa!" someone called in a quiet moment.

"Oh my goodness," said Clarissa. "There are so many that I don't know where to begin!" But begin she did, and she was delighted with all of the gifts the dolls had made.

"Thank you all so much," she said again and again. "I never knew a birthday could be so wonderful!"

Sometimes in all the excitement of a birthday it's hard to remember to say "thank you" for everything. When it is your birthday, take special care to thank everyone who brings you something!

When the cake had been eaten and the presents opened, Raggedy Ann stood up.

"Shall we play some birthday party games?" All the other dolls cheered. Raggedy Ann always knew the best games.

Many fun party games must be set up in advance. This takes a little extra work, but it's worth it! Try to keep your games simple, and, if you can, have plenty of small toys as prizes so that everyone wins something.

On the next few pages, you will learn how to prepare for and play some of Raggedy Ann's favorite party games.

PIN THE TAIL ON THE DONKEY

How to prepare:

Draw or paint a donkey (or any animal you like) on a large piece of paper. Do not draw a tail on the animal! Next, draw or paint several tails on separate pieces of paper and cut them out. Put a loop of tape on the back of each tail. Find a wall where there is not much furniture around, and tape your animal there at about shoulder level.

How to play:

Let all the players see where the animal is taped and where the tail belongs. Give each player a tail. One by one, tie a blindfold (a scarf works well) on the players and let them try to "pin" the tail on the animal. Each player should start several steps away from the wall. Sometimes you can even spin the player around a few times first to make it harder. Whoever pins the tail closest to the right spot wins a prize!

SPIDER WEB

How to prepare:

Count how many people will be at the party and gather that many balls of yarn. (If each ball is a different color, you will have a beautiful rainbow web!) Tie a small prize or treat to the end of each ball, and hide the treats in different places around a large room. Then stretch the yarn from each ball all over the room, looping around furniture and zigzagging high and low. Make each ball of yarn end at the doorway. Now it might be impossible to walk through the room!

How to play:

Each player chooses a piece of yarn. When everyone is ready, the players begin to follow their yarn, winding it back up into a ball as they go. Players might have to do some ducking or stretching to make their way through the web! Soon, though, everyone will find a prize, and you will be able to walk through the room again.

MYSTERY PRESENT

How to prepare:

Gather as many kinds of wrapping paper as you can. It's a good idea to use paper that you've saved from old presents, and don't forget about newspaper, aluminum foil, and brown paper bags! Wrap a small prize. Then put the present in a small cardboard box and wrap it again in a different kind of paper. Then wrap it again, and then again, and then again, using more boxes if you have them. Don't waste *too* much paper, but keep wrapping until you have a good-sized package wrapped in at least as many layers as you will have players.

How to play:

The players sit in a circle. One person starts by unwrapping the first layer of paper. The present is then passed to the next person, who opens the next layer. Whoever opens the final layer solves the mystery and wins the prize!

"There," said Raggedy Ann as all the dolls finished cleaning up cake crumbs and crumpled wrapping paper. "Now you know what birthdays are all about!"

"What a happy day!" said Clarissa. She has had a lovely time with her new friends, and they all have enjoyed her birthday, too. "I must say I am sorry I have to wait a whole year for my birthday to come around again!"

"We will celebrate other birthdays before then," said Raggedy Ann with a smile.

"Many happy birthdays to you all!"